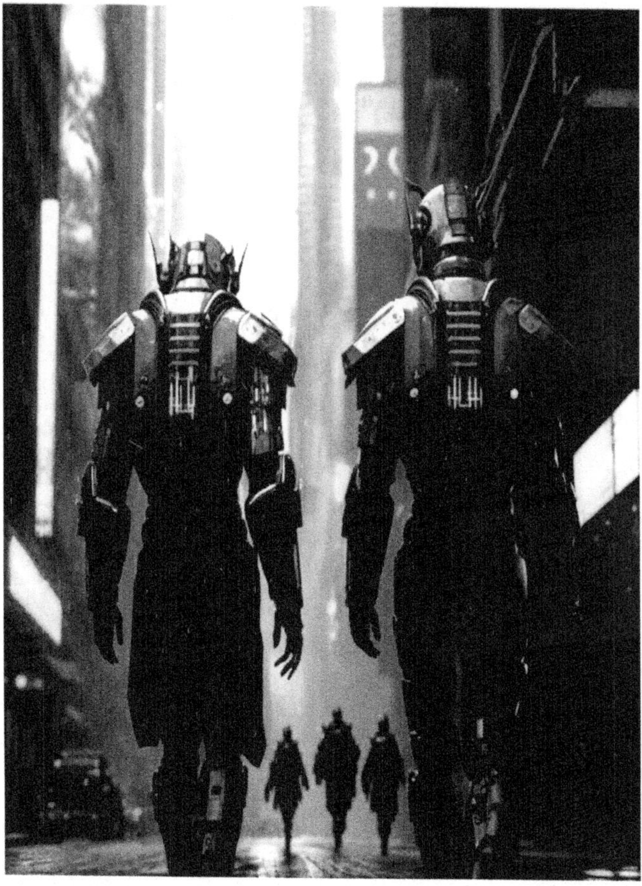

Copyright © 2023 Zinaida Kirko
All rights reserved.
No portion of this book may be reproduced in any form without written permission from the publisher or author, except as permitted by U.S. copyright law.

On the twin planets of Verta and Vouna, which have become overwhelmed with garbage, chaos reigns, and everyone has lost hope that their lives can be improved. Father and son descend to the bottom of the ocean and find something they have never seen before, which may be the hope for a brighter future…

W712

Zinaida Kirko

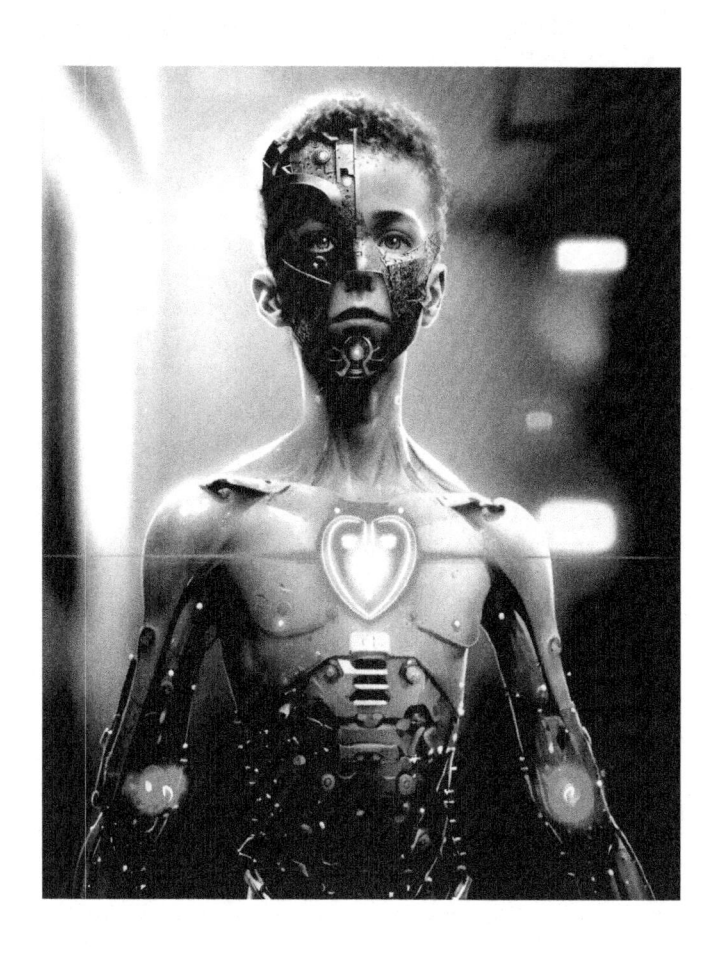

1

Orca

Chapter 1.

The Orca sank lower and lower in a place where the ocean bed was very deep.

It looked like a copper-colored egg-shaped capsule. It moved with agility and speed.

"Look, dad, there's something there!" Joey exclaimed.

The boy and his father Pran clung to the porthole of the submarine.

They were approaching the bottom and now it was already possible to make out what it was - it looked like the seabed was strewn with piles of garbage.

"It can't be," Pran took off his glasses and sighed in disappointment.

Joey just wrinkled his nose and leaned even closer to the glass.

"Not only is the entire surface of the planet covered with garbage, but also down here," Pran turned away.

"No dad, look!"

Pran chuckled in disbelief.

"It's not just trash!"

They started looking at it again. The sea bed was covered not with rubbish but with discarded robots – or more precisely, parts of them.

The Orca held out its long, springy arms. It lifted the bodies, heads, arms, and the legs in turn, bringing them closer to the porthole in order to be viewed in detail.

"Just think," said Pran. "These are what was once artificial intelligence!"

Joey broke into a smile and his eyes lit up. "But they were not just dumped here...

at the bottom of the ocean, right?"

"Yes, you are right to be puzzled," Pran nodded his head. "They must have had a very good reason for doing such a thing."

Suddenly, Orca grunted and shuddered. The lights went out, and the submarine flopped into a pile of scrap metal.

⊕

Blockages

Chapter 2.

Pran and Joey found themselves in total darkness. It extended far beyond their submarine. Both realized this instantly, as well as the fact that it was impossible to overcome this darkness without the help of the Orca's power.

"I think the engine is dead," Pran said calmly, "though it shouldn't have been. I checked it a hundred times the night before."

Joey was groping in the dark for the emergency engine start button. He found it and turned on the light.

"It won't last long, will it?"

"For a couple of hours. But during this time, I think I will be able to fix the power module."

They both put on diving suits and went outside.

The Orca was lying on its side like a wounded animal and was spitting bubbles of air into the darkness.

Pran opened her side and began to repair the motor.

"I'll walk around here for a while," Joey said.

His father waved his hand, and the boy moved through the rubble, which spread in all directions like skyscrapers in a dead city.

He had never seen so many broken robots in one place. They lay in every orientation with twisted faces frozen forever.

Suddenly, amid all this rubbish, something shone and caught his eye. Joey turned around to check if Orca was still there as he didn't want to go too far. After all, getting lost in the cemetery of robots at the bottom of the ocean is not a very pleasant prospect. However, he wondered what could shine at such depth?

He looked at the device on his wrist and took a deep breath.

"Just a little more than enough oxygen to go back," he thought, and, having made up his mind, stepped even further into the depths.

Alive

Chapter 3.

The darkness thickened and at some point closed in a dense wall behind the boy. Joey's heart skipped a beat as he realized this. Now, all he saw was just a dot of light, flickering somewhere ahead.

It was too late to retreat. Joey moved forward, ignoring his fear. Finally, he got close enough to see. The dot was bright scarlet. A heart? Joey looked puzzled. It appeared to be the heart of one of the robots that had been surrounded by metal debris. It was still beating. Alive? But how was it possible? After all, he has laid here for an eternity. Where did he get the energy from?

Joey looked around again - the Orca was no longer visible. Now he didn't even know where it was. Left? Or right? He tried not to think about it. Carefully he began to free the robot. Leaving him here would be wrong. He needed to show his dad this perpetual motion machine.

Joey had spent several minutes pulling him out of the rubble when suddenly something violently knocked him off his feet. He turned around and immediately realized that it was a Shtikha - a kind of shark with tentacles like an octopus. To meet one at the bottom of the ocean, especially outside of your submarine, is certain death.

The boy glanced at the rubble again. He had almost released the scarlet heart robot.

"Leave me, Joey," he suddenly heard and shuddered, "save yourself!"

Where did this sound come from? It was clearly audible through the headphones. But it was not Pran.

The Shtikha turned around and showed its five rows of teeth in a ferocious grin. It then started attacking again. Joey had to leave to save himself, but then changed his mind and quickly grabbed the robot by the arm and pulled it with force. The Shtikha approached and Joey closed his eyes.

When he opened them, he found himself lying next to the Orca. His father stood and looked down at him, and on his right - there was a robot with a fire-like heart.

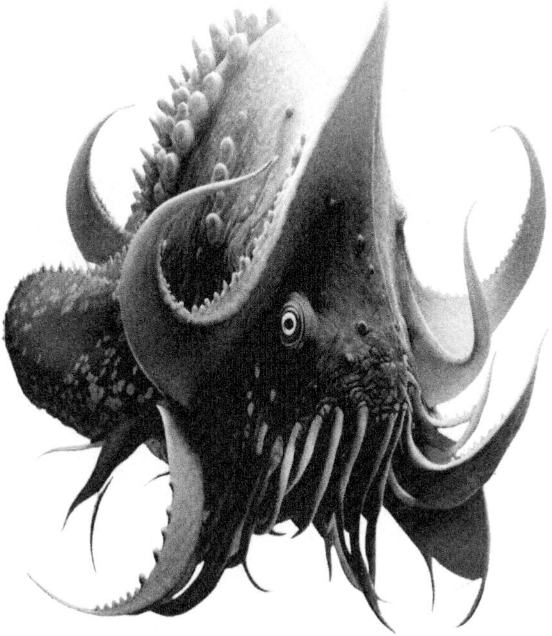

Friend of all people

Chapter 4.

"He knew my name!" Joey said as they drank a vitamin smoothie back at the Orca. Pran had fixed it and it was as good as new. "I tell you, at first he talked to me, called me by name, and then saved me!"

"You say you heard it in your headphones?"
"Yes! Clearly, just like you!"

The robot sat on the floor and its scarlet heart continued to beat. He was only knee-high but looked like a man. Only the leather covering and paint had peeled off in a few places, exposing the metal. He had "W712" scratched into his shoulder with a sharp object.

"Very interesting," Pran could not take his eyes off him, "he takes energy from nowhere. So... he really is alive."

"We should take him with us!"
"No, we can't, it's forbidden!"
"But why, dad? Why do we even go down to such a depth then?"

"To explore the ocean floor! But this," Pran lowered his voice, "can be dangerous... very dangerous... A living robot at a great depth. No wonder they put him here! He's probably really dangerous!"

"W712, talk to us," Joey asked, turning to the robot, "tell us who you are and where you are from."

The robot opened its eyes.

"Pran doesn't want to take me with him, Joey. There are probably reasons for this."

The father turned pale.

"Who are you?" he barked demandingly, "and how do you know our names?"

W712 blinked.

"I don't remember," he answered. "Those who put me at the bottom of the ocean erased my memory. All I remember is that I am the Friend of All People."

"We should take him with us," Joey insisted.

"It is forbidden," Pran repeated again.

But Joey noticed how he froze and turned even paler when W712 looked at him point-blank. Then Pran turned away and went to the porthole.

"All right," he said finally.

"Did he say something to you, dad? You heard it in your headphones, right?" Joey asked.

"Maybe you are right," Pran smiled slightly and patted the boy on the head. "You should not leave a friend of all people on the seabed."

⊕

Verta and Vouna

Chapter 5.

Five suns and three moons illuminated Verta and Vouna with soft light from all sides. These artificial planets were built many hundreds of thousands of years ago by brilliant architects of their time. They were connected by a bridge and they twisted around each other as if in a dance to create gravity.

Pran moored the Orca in the Inverted Port. It was so called because the water coming out of the ocean hung in the air by design so that the boats were on top and did not interfere with anyone below.

The father and the boy went down the stairs and looked up. W712 took a few awkward steps and looked around.

He narrowed his eyes against the light of the suns. And then looked around the surface of the planet, which was covered with piles of debris. People lived amongst it, built houses, and no one even thought that it could be otherwise.

"I seem to remember something," said W712, "but I don't remember what…"

"You'll have plenty of time to catch up," Joey smiled.

The robot followed them. He turned his head 360 degrees, looking at everything around him.

"He's kind of weird," Pran whispered, "not like modern robots."

"I was at the bottom of the ocean for one hundred and fifteen thousand and forty-four years, 2 months, ten days, three hours, and two minutes," the robot said, "and then Joey found me."

"Wow," the boy exclaimed. "I wonder what our planets were like in those days?"

All three stopped when several robots blocked their path. These were the Plunes, the ultimate representatives of robotic artificial intelligence today. Everyone knew that in ancient times they kept order. But now it wasn't so. Now the Plunes only sowed fear and chaos, creating conflicts, not solving them. People have long forgotten how to subjugate them. And over time, they seized power on both planets, and overpowered the people.

"What is it?" they asked, pointing to W712.

"I am the Friend of All People," the robot explained.

The Plunes looked at each other, and then laughed mockingly.

"Did you find it in the ocean?" If so, then we should confiscate it.

"No," Pran waved his hand. "What ocean? I spent a lot of time making a toy for my son for his twelfth birthday."

The Plunes looked at the robot suspiciously. "What can he do?"

"He says everything out of place, that's all."

"Say something," they demanded.

"The planet is littered," W712 said sternly.

"Is he trying to insult us?" exclaimed Plunes.

They were responsible, among other things, for order in the city. At least that's how it was thought.

"No," Pran began to make excuses again, "I'm telling you, I didn't finish it."

"Leave them," said the senior robot, "the piece of metal is really not worth our attention. But if you don't manage to fix it, both you and that heap of junk will end up in the ocean! I doubt you will be able to return from there."

They laughed again and moved on.

$\oplus$

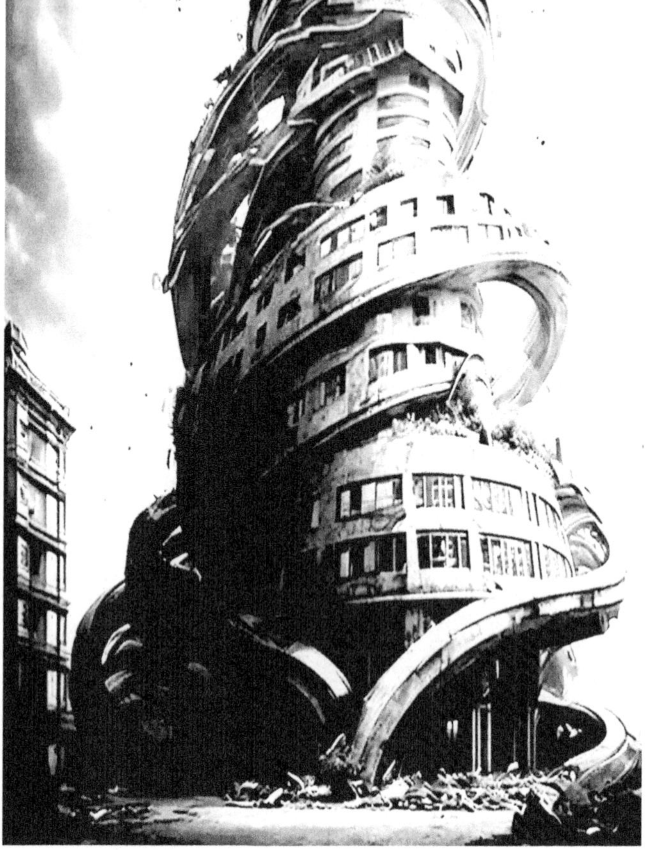

Ancient Library

Chapter 6.

Everything was the same in the house on Diagonal Street. Neighbors were boiling seaweed, the smell of which infested the entire neighborhood. Pran was cleaning his suits while Joey was asking W712 questions. However, as it turned out, the robot really did not remember anything.

"What if I take him to the hall of the tablets?" Joey suddenly exclaimed, "because all the information about our past is stored there."

"Great idea," agreed Pran, "but you know that all knowledge has been lost too long."

"Not so long ago, now that we have W712 to help! Will he remember though?"

"Very well," agreed Pran. "But be careful not to get caught by the Plunes. You never know what's on their mind."

Joey hid the W712 in his backpack and went outside. They walked through the streets and moving walk-ways, which weaved over the city in circles, and passed through piles and piles of rubbish. Having strayed among the streets, they finally came to an abandoned quarter.

"It's dangerous to be here," the robot said, looking at the skewed houses through a hole in the backpack.

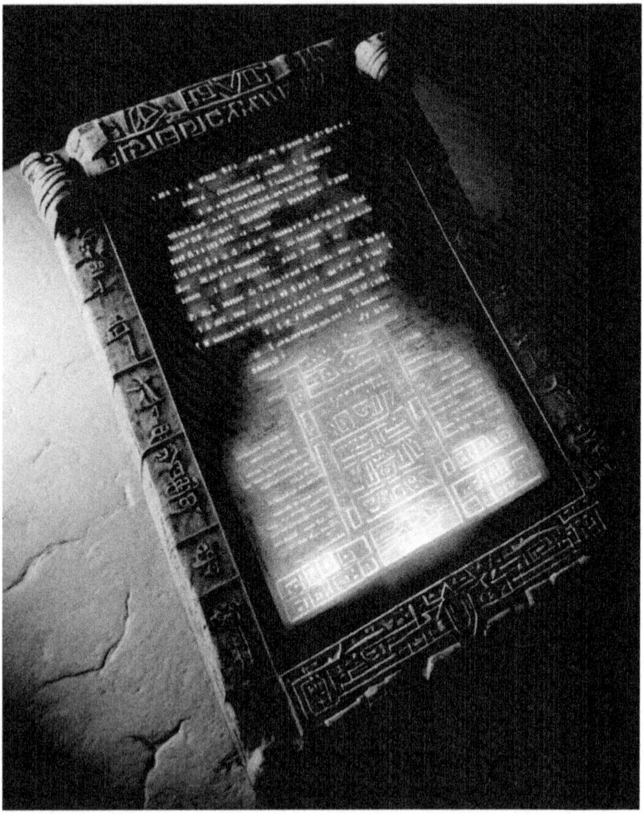

"No more than in any other part of the city," said Joey. "No one comes here, because here is the Ancient Library. Which, unfortunately, is completely useless."

He took out the W712 and put it on the ground. The robot tilted its head up, trying to see the roof of the tall ugly building in front of it. But it was out of sight as the spiraling tower of the Library headed into the clouds.

"Why is this building useless? I have identified that within this building resides the largest amount of data in all the city."

"Yes, there is data, but no one can decipher it." and continued to move forward through the dilapidated archway to the entrance.

⊕

Forgotten past

Chapter 7.

Joey and W712 opened the rickety door and stepped inside. Just like outside, the walls inside twisted in a spiral and went upwards as far as the eye could see. And on the walls, stretched endless shelves filled with transparent tablets. The tablets were not only on the shelves, they were everywhere. They hung in the air and spun, flying around the hall. The floor of the library was covered with garbage, and several people wandered aimlessly around.

"Why is valuable data so devalued?" asked W712.

"Because for a hundred thousand years no one has been able to read them," Joey shrugged and moved further up the stairs.

"So you don't know anything about your past?"

"No," Joey answered, "only stories and legends of Street Teachers. They are so nicknamed because they claim to know something. But I don't believe in it."

They went out to the balcony.

"They say that earlier there was no garbage on Verta and Vouna, can you imagine?" Joey laughed.

"Indeed, that is true," W712 picked up one of the tablets, spinning in the air. "Why don't you read what is written here?"

"I can't, no one can."

"It says here that the planets were designed to be green and healthy," W712 said.

Joey jumped up and down.

"Can you read them?"

But he immediately covered his mouth and looked around. And then he took the robot aside.

"Nobody has to know, okay?" he whispered. "What else is written there?"

W712 took the tablet in his hands, and then a beam lit up from his eyes, scanning it. At that moment, Verta and Vouna appeared in front of them, spinning in the air dancing together in outer space. But they were not at all what they are now. They were green and blooming and had no debris on them at all.

"Wow! How do you do it?!" Joey exclaimed.

"I don't know," the robot shrugged.

The beams from his eyes scanned the entire library.

"I have read them all," said W712, "now I know a lot about your past."

Joey's eyes lit up.

"You must tell us! Tell all the inhabitants of our world!"

However, Joey immediately fell silent. Plunes came out from around the corner. Among them was the leader Bragan. It was said that nothing in the city happened without his knowledge. He was thin and tall, and the pale waxy skin of his long face made him look like a dead man.

"How interesting," he said and squatted down in front of W712. "So you really are from the bottom of the ocean..."

W712 stepped back and hid behind Joey.

The time has come

Chapter 8.

Bragan smiled, revealing crooked teeth. The rest of the Plunes laughed.

"Did you and your father think you could hide such a find from me?" he grabbed the robot and twisted his hands. "Now all the knowledge in this library will belong to us."

"These tablets should belong to everyone!" Joey exclaimed indignantly.

"But they've always belonged to you, haven't they?" objected Bragan. "But you never took them!"

With these words, he moved away from the library, taking W712 with him. And the Plunes held Joey until their leader was out of sight.

The boy ran home as fast as he could, and then flew into the apartment and slammed the door behind him.

"They took W712!" he exclaimed with tears in his eyes"

Pran hugged his son and sighed.

"I warned you that such a find could be dangerous if picked up from the bottom of the ocean. Not so much because it holds great potential, but because it can fall into the wrong hands."

22

"He knows everything! Everything that is written in the tablets," Joey exclaimed. "We must help him before the Plunes harm him!"

But neither father nor son could figure out how. They didn't even know where he was.

Joey walked around the apartment sad all day. All night he could not sleep, watching the three moons dance in the sky. But the next morning at breakfast, he remembered something.

"Why did you change your mind then, at the bottom of the ocean?" he asked Pran.

"He said," Pran replied, "that... the time has come. That's what your mum always said. I don't know how he knew that... just like our names."

"But what does this mean?"

"Your mother always said that when I couldn't decide on something important."

"The time has come," repeated Joey. "Yes, but this time not only for us, but for both planets! We cannot sit idly by! We must do something!"

With these words, he got up and ran out into the street. And Pran followed him.

$\oplus$

Star sailor

Chapter 9.

The part of the city where the Plunes lived was on a hill and was the richest, despite the fact that it was also built on garbage. The Plunes, as representatives of power, built tall luxurious houses, showing off their superiority. That's where Joey and Pran decided to go.

"If they want to hide the W712, then this is where it will be," the boy concluded.

"But what if we get caught?" said the father, "besides, even if we find a robot, how can we get him out of there?"

"I have an idea," Joey exclaimed, "let's drop in on Phuey!"

Phuey was a star sailor. That's what everyone called him. The inhabitants of Verta and Vouna have never been in space. But there were stories and legends about those times gone by when any inhabitant of the planets could go to the stars. Phuey believed it too. He built majestic ships out of junk. However, he lacked knowledge and therefore all of them had one drawback - they could not actually reach the stars.

When Joey and Pran entered the spacious courtyard, they immediately began to examine the aircrafts, built from old pieces of iron, cans, lids, pots, and gears.

And Phuey came out to meet them. He was a bit stout, with a grey beard, a long mustache, and cheerful eyes that were covered with several pairs of spectacles.

"Ah, my good old friends!" Phuey exclaimed joyfully.

"Just don't say that you want to go into space!"

"No, not so far this time. However, we need your help," Pran replied.

And they told Phuey about everything that had happened.

"They kidnapped a robot with a scarlet heart, a friend of all people who knows everything about our past!"

Phuey's indignation could not be hidden and he immediately began looking for a suitable craft for them.

"It should not be too small, not too big, but it should be the best."

"Here...This!" exclaimed the shipbuilder as he pointed to one of his creations. "It's unlikely to reach the stars, but it will circle over the planets as much as it wants!"

After thanking him, Pran and Joey boarded the aircraft, but they noticed that Phuey looked very sad.

"What happened?" they asked.

"Hurry up," said the shipbuilder, "otherwise the Plunes will dismantle the W712 for parts. They always do this when they don't understand what they're facing.
And then no one will know either about him or about the past of our planets."

The boy and his father thanked Phuey the shipbuilder and took to the air.

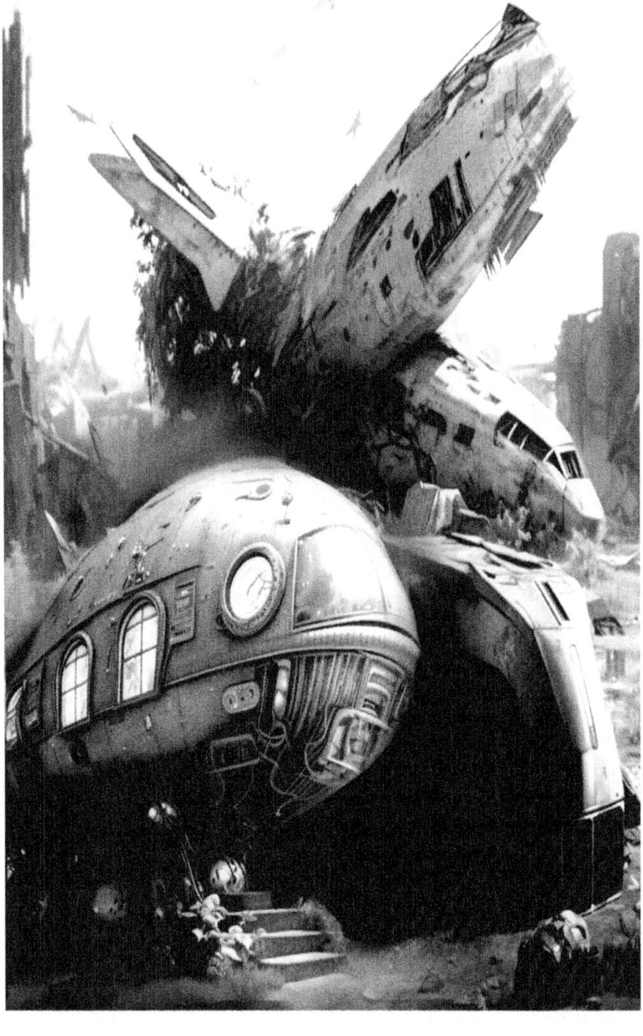

Escape

Chapter 10.

Joey and Pran flew over the city and looked at the endless piles of garbage around. The boy told his father about how their planets used to be. They both tried to imagine how wonderful it would be if Verta and Vouna were clean and green again.

They soon landed near the Plunes' quarter and decided to consider a plan of action.

"Now we need to find W712," Joey said.

"But how?" Pran wondered.

"He can transmit thoughts directly to our headphones!"

The boy closed his eyes and called W712.

"I'm here," he immediately heard and clapped his hands happily.

"He hears me!"

W712 described to them where he was. They flew up to the tallest house on the hill and landed on its roof.

"He seems to be here."

Joey and Pran opened the rooftop door and went downstairs. But the Plunes immediately blocked their path. They grabbed them and took them to the hall where Bragan was sitting. And next to him was W712, tied up.

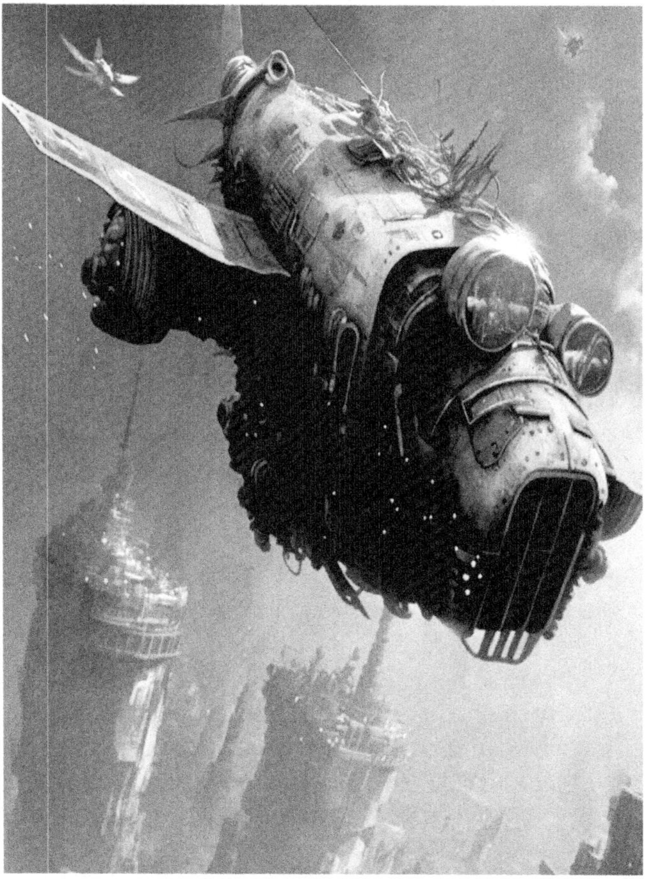

"Yeah, here they are, the explorers of the ocean floor," said Bragan. "It's about time you appeared. Your friend," he pointed to the robot, "is not too talkative, but you must certainly tell us about everything that you found on the seabed and everything that your friend is silent about, otherwise we will have to take him apart!"

"It is highly discouraged to disclose information to these individuals," W712 blurted out.

The Plunes immediately tied up the robot's mouth.

"Everything in this city," said Bragan, "as well as everything on these planets belongs to the Plunes. This includes your robot friend and all the knowledge of the Ancient Library."

"No, all this belongs to the inhabitants of Verta and Vouna!" objected Joey, " and you can not stop us!"

With these words, he broke free from their tight grip and untied the robot. And W712 hit the Plunes with some kind of vibrational wave so that they fell to the floor, confused.

Pran, Joey, and the robot made their way back onto the roof. They ran to the aircraft and climbed in. They then soared into the air with such speed that the Plunes would hardly have had time to catch up with them.

Heart of Verta and Vouna

Chapter 11.

How happy Joey and Pran were when the W712 was with them again. He told them how the Plunes tried to get him to talk, but he didn't tell them anything. He also explained that it is extremely dangerous to tell them anything since all their programs are malfunctioning. So his higher intellect told him.

"I translated the information of the Ancient Library into your language so that everyone can read it," said W712 and handed Joey a small disk. "Now the knowledge will return to your world!"

Joey and Pran couldn't contain their happiness. They flew over the garbage cities and rose higher and higher.

"There is something else I have to tell you," said W712, "when I was reading the tablets about the history of your world, I came across one of them... and it seemed special to me."

"What is it about?" Joey asked impatiently.

"It's about the fact that at the bottom of the ocean lies the lost heart of your world, the heart of Verta and Vouna. And without it, your planets have been dying for many thousands of years. But what if... just imagine what if you found it?"

"So you mean," Pran asked, "that you are the heart of our world?"

"When I read this... I remembered," said W712, "that this is exactly what I am! And your world is fading because I'm misplaced."

"How can we get you back to where you need to be?" Joey asked.

"We must fly to the bridge, where Verta and Vouna merge together. That is where their common heart should be."

Pran and Joey donned their space suits and took off.

New World

Chapter 12.

Phuey's Flying Machine crackled louder and louder as they rose above the planets heading towards the bridge.

They soon landed. Here the planets Verta and Vouna merged together, and at their junction, there was a mountain. Pran, Joey, and W712 approached it.

"Your planets were created artificially, but they have a living heart. This is where it should be," said the robot and extended his hand.

The mountain opened up, and they went inside a huge hall with many appliances and fixtures. In the middle was a hollow in the shape of W712. The robot smiled, waved goodbye to them, stood in this cavity, and disappeared into it.

Joey and Pran did not have time to come to their senses, as a loud thunderous roar began. The boy could not believe that the robot had disappeared and did not want to move, but Pran pulled him along. They ran outside and boarded the aircraft again.

They flew high enough to watch the world change before their eyes. It turned green and came to life, turning into what W712 showed Joey in the Ancient Library.

When they landed, they saw that the piles of debris were gradually disappearing, dissolving, and turning into dust.

"Have the planets launched a self-cleaning system?" Pran exclaimed.

"Dad, look!" Joey pointed down at the city.

They couldn't believe their eyes. The Plunes went around picking up dust and leftover debris, putting the planet in order.

"W712 reprogrammed them!"

The once ugly buildings were turned into neat houses, and the streets were straight and beautiful. The inhabitants of Verta and Vouna walked around, inhaling the fresh clean air and looked at everything around with surprise.

But Joey and Pran were sad. Their friend had merged with the planet. However, they understood that he left behind a New World for all of us.

"Pran, Joey," they suddenly heard in their headphones and both of them jumped in place, "the planets are returning to their original form," W712 said, "there is nothing to worry about. Only a bright future lies ahead!"

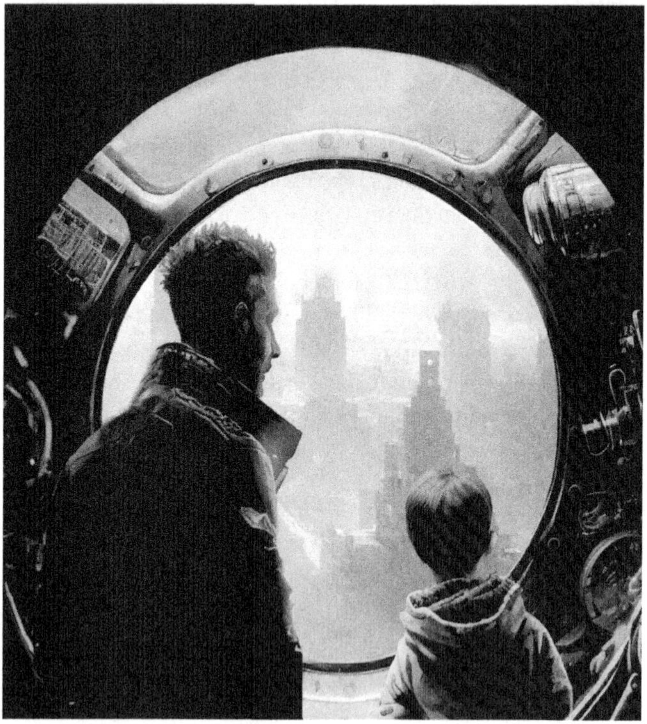

Thank you reading this book!

This is our small family business where everyone has their role: Zinaida Kirko - author, Victoria Harwood - author, illustrator and promoter, Igor Kirko - editor, Leslie Harwood - translator.

We highly recommend you to explore our other captivating books, Dream World and Dragon Island, which are filled with thrilling tales of fantastical adventures!

Printed in Great Britain
by Amazon